Ladybird Readers

Let's Find the Treasure!

To access the audio and digital versions
of this book:

1 Go to www.ladybirdeducation.co.uk
2 Click "Unlock book"
3 Enter the code below

tkAJydSWXe

Notes to teachers, parents, and carers

The *Ladybird Readers* Beginner level helps young language learners to become familiar with key conversational phrases in English. The language introduced has clear real-life applications, giving children the tools to hold their first conversations in English.

This book focuses on asking the question "Where is . . .?" and provides practice of answering "Yes" and "No" in English. The pictures that accompany the text show a range of settings, which may be used to introduce one or two pieces of topic-based vocabulary, such as "fox" and "sheep", if the children are ready.

There are some activities to do in this book. They will help children practice these skills:

Speaking   Listening*   Writing   Reading   Singing*

*To complete these activities, listen to the audio downloads available at www.ladybirdeducation.co.uk

Aardman

Series Editor: Sorrel Pitts   Text adapted by Hazel Geatches   Song lyrics by Wardour Studios

LADYBIRD BOOKS

UK | USA | Canada | Ireland | Australia
India | New Zealand | South Africa

Ladybird Books is part of the Penguin Random House group of companies whose addresses can be found at global.penguinrandomhouse.com.
www.penguin.co.uk   www.puffin.co.uk   www.ladybird.co.uk

Penguin
Random House
UK

First published 2021
001

Printed in China
A CIP catalogue record for this book is available from the British Library
ISBN: 978-0-241-44009-4

All correspondence to:
Ladybird Books
Penguin Random House Children's
One Embassy Gardens, 8 Viaduct Gardens, London SW11 7BW

MIX
Paper from
responsible sources
FSC® C018179
FSC
www.fsc.org

Ladybird Readers

Let's Find
the Treasure!

Based on the Learning Time with Timmy TV series
created in partnership with the British Council

Watch the original episode "Find the Treasure" online.

LEARN MORE!

Watch on ▶ YouTube

YouTube /LearningTimeWithTimmy
LearningTimeWithTimmy.com

Picture words

Timmy

Finlay

Ruffy

 treasure map

 treasure

 vegetable garden

 sandpit

Timmy has a treasure map.

Where is the treasure?
Let's find it!

Is the treasure in the vegetable garden?

9

Finlay looks in the vegetable garden.

Does he find the treasure?
No!

Is the treasure in the flower garden?

Ruffy looks in the flower garden.

Does he find the treasure?
No!

Is the treasure in the sandpit?
Ruffy and Timmy look in
the sandpit.

Do they find the treasure?

Yes, they find the treasure!

18

Well done, Ruffy and Timmy!

1 Talk with a friend.

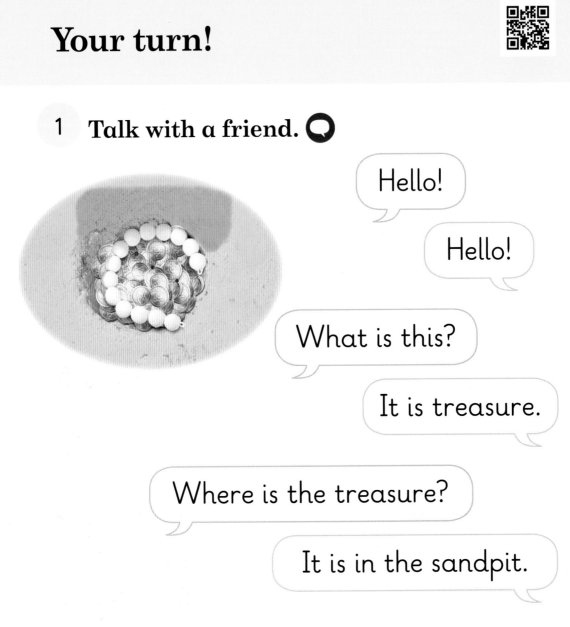

Hello!

Hello!

What is this?

It is treasure.

Where is the treasure?

It is in the sandpit.

2 Listen and read. Match. 🎧 📖

1 Timmy has a treasure map.

2 Finlay looks in the vegetable garden.

3 Ruffy and Timmy find the treasure.

3 What color? Listen. Circle the words. 🎧 📖

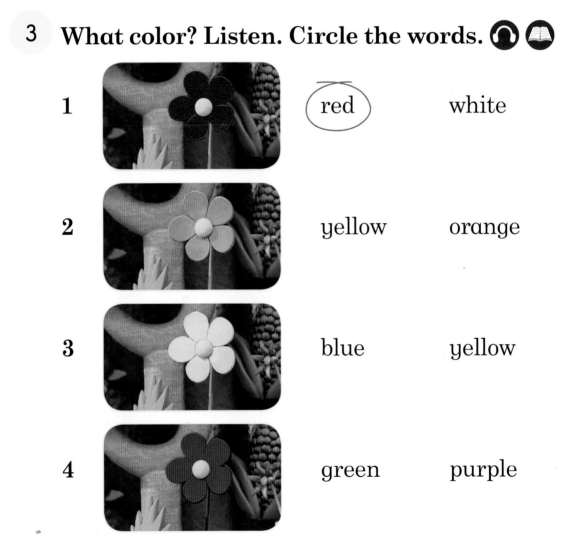

1   red   white

2   yellow   orange

3   blue   yellow

4   green   purple

22

4 Listen. Write the first letters.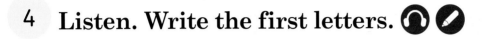

1  sandpit

2  map

3  garden

5 Sing the song. 🎵

Let's find the treasure! Let's find the treasure!
Is the treasure in the sandpit?
Let's find the treasure! Let's find the treasure!
Can you find it?

Let's look in the flower garden.
Let's look in the vegetable garden.
Let's look in the sandpit.
Timmy has a treasure map!
Timmy has a treasure map!

Let's find the treasure! Let's find the treasure!
Is the treasure in the sandpit?
Let's find the treasure! Let's find the treasure!
Can you find it?